WITHDRAWN

The Kiddie Table

by Colleen Madden

CAPSTONE EDITIONS

a capstone imprint

One Thanksgiving ...

. . . a girl who had just turned eight,
a bit tallish for her years,
dressed in sequins and flowers
with silver acorns in her ears,
was told to sit at the kiddie table.

Not quite a teen
but no longer a tot,
she wondered why the adults
hadn't saved her a spot.

So there she sat, like a little kid,
with a bowl and a spoon
and a cup with a lid.

"Is this for real?"
the girl asked out loud.
"Why am I stuck
with this pacifier crowd?"

Then her cousin Willie
plopped potatoes on her thigh.
She glared at the dining room,
trying not to cry.

"This ISN'T FAIR! This ISN'T cool!
To make me spend Thanksgiving
with kids who burp and drool!"

The girl jumped up from her chair
and started to shout.
"If this is a joke,
YOU BETTER CUT IT RIGHT OUT!

I can eat pickled beets!
I don't need them strained!
And unlike these little ones
I AM POTTY TRAINED!"

"I can easily do two-digit multiplication,
and I earned my swimming badge
last summer vacation.
I make my own waffles.
I use the microwave!
I can sit at the big table.
I know how to behave!"

"I KNOW
how to use
a fork!

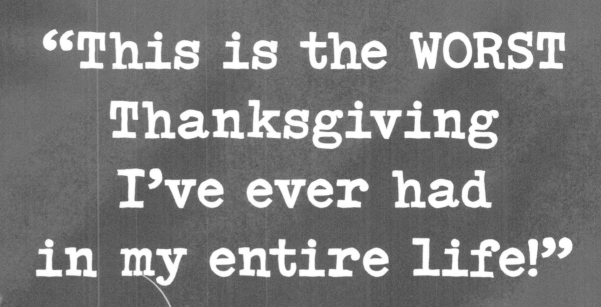

"This is the WORST Thanksgiving I've ever had in my entire life!"

I DESERVE A SPOT AT THE ADULT TABLE!

SHLOOOOOOOP!

The quiet was loud,
but mom saved the day.
Thankfully moms always
know what to say.

"You're too old to sit with babies.
I see what you mean.
You are at a tough age.
You're stuck in between.

Next time please ask me
if you'd rather sit with us.
Don't yell across the kitchen
and create such a fuss.

I'll make you a spot
at the dining room table.
Clean up and calm down,
and join us when you're able."

Pumpkin soup was served
in special bowls from France.
The girl told her cousin
all about Irish dance.

After dinner's end,
her parents got a huge hug and kiss.
For she felt like such a grown-up,
a big girl's one true wish!

She helped wash the dishes,
gave out leftovers in totes.
Then she bundled up the babies
into their little coats.

She said goodbye,
feeling just a bit sad.
For as Thanksgivings go,
this one wasn't so bad.

And NEXT Thanksgiving ...

... if you remember to ask
but the big table is jammed,
wear a top and old jeans
and lose the girly glam.

Be **THANKFUL** for family,
fun, and growing up.
And sit at the kiddie table
without a sippy cup!

**For my mom, who sometimes let me eat in the kitchen
with the dogs and made every holiday something
to remember and write about one day. -Colleen**

The Kiddie Table is published by
Capstone Editions, a Captone imprint
1710 Roe Crest Drive, North Mankato, Minnesota 56003
www.mycapstone.com

Library of Congress Cataloging-in-Publication data
is available on the Library of Congress website.

ISBN: 978-1-68446-002-1

Designer: Ashlee Suker

Printed and bound in the USA.
PA021